THE GIRL, THE ROCKER, AND THE TOWN

MIRACLE:
THE MILAGRO IN TAFTICOPA

By: Vittorio Nolan Wyatt Gray

The Girl, The Rocker, and The Town: Miracle The Milagro in Tafticopa

Vittorio Wyatt Gray

Published by Vittorio Wyatt Gray, 2024.

---

1. http://www.vittoriowyattgray.com/

THE GIRL, THE ROCKER, AND THE TOWN: MIRACLE THE MILAGRO IN TAFTICOPA

First edition. July 20, 2024.

ISBN: 979-8227400123

Written by Vittorio Wyatt Gray.

Table of Contents

<u>**Acknowledgements:**</u>
The author would like to thank the city of Maricopa, CA and the City of Taft, CA, as well as Taft College, Professor Golling, Alice P. Hughes, the Gray family, and his loving wife.

<u>Prologue:</u>

Tafticopa, CA is a small town located between Taft, and Maricopa. It is a sandy oilfield town with huge farms on the outskirts. Many of the residents have lived there for generations and came over after the Dust Bowl forced people to move west.

It is the kind of town that feels like it is in a time capsule in some ways. Old buildings from the early 1900s line the historic downtown streets, while newer business and bright tomorrows are located just a few streets over.

Leon Picante is somewhere in between. Owned by the Leon family, an All-American, hot dog eating, salsa making family started by the grandparents, Rogelio and Lupita. They migrated here from Puerto Juan, a small island in the Caribbean a long time ago looking for better opportunities, but never finalized their citizenship. That did not stop them from raising a beautiful family, sending their son off to fight in the war, and opening up a small hacienda style restaurant that has been a centerpointe of the community for years. Birthdays, holidays, and celebrations of all kinds have been held at Leon Picante. Many memories made.

The whole world has been shut down by the global pandemic. People are urged to socially distance, stay home when possible, and wear a mask. Certain items are still not available on the shelves many months in, though people are learning to live with the new reality.

Small businesses are stretched very thin. The customers just don't come in like they used to and many businesses are finding it hard to stay afloat. Leon Picante is one of those small businesses. Many that applied for assistance from the government are beginning to receive their funds, but Rogelio and Lupita do not qualify.

The pandemic is forcing neighbors to support neighbors, and families to stick together to get through. People cling more strongly to their faith as a means of survival. The hope of things one day getting better. It is in these difficult times that our story begins.

CHAPTER 1

The Calling

"Oh, what a magical night!" thought Marta as she listened to music through her headphones while sitting at her computer desk. She was listening to a song by her favorite rock star, Slate 'Skastar' Cruddy and his band, The Muggy Hamsters. She and her best friends, Katrina and Courtney attended a Slate and The Muggy Hamsters concert two years ago when Marta was lucky caller number fourteen in the 97.3 Tafticopa Jams - Guess This Noise contest and won three front row tickets.

> *"Do you believe in equality? Yeah! Do you believe that we all are free? Yeah! I believe in you, do you believe in me? I hope you do, let's protest peacefully, with love, love, love, love, love, love, love. With love, love, love, love, love, love, love..."*

She closed her mind to the outside world and was transported back in her memory to the night of that concert, and the moment that Slate's bracelet flew off of his wrist and landed right in her hands.

"Do it with love, love, love, love, love, love, love".

She remembered Katrina and Courtney's faces as she caught the bracelet, and Slate motioned for her to come on stage at the end of the song. She also remembered how her heart was beating out of her chest just knowing that she would get to meet the rock star she adored since 8th grade face to face. She walked up the stairs of the creaky little stage and almost slipped backwards when Slate grabbed her hand, and pulled her to himself.

"Thank you for returning my bracelet," said Slate. "It cost me 5 thousand dollars!"

Marta was in so much awe of the rocker that she could not think of a single word to say, and just stood there with a giddy wide-eyed smile on her face.

"What's your name?" he asked her. She was still so excited, but she couldn't stand there and say nothing forever.

"Marta" she excitedly replied, "Marta Ramona Leon!" Slate reached in his guitar case behind the speaker, pulled out a small poster with his picture on it, and began to sign it.

"Well, Marta Ramona Leon," he said as he was writing, "if you ever need a favor, I owe you one." Courtney and Katrina looked on as Marta's knees almost buckled when Slate looked her in the eye, and handed her the autograph. He grabbed her hand again, and led her down the stairs and back to her two best friends.

"OMG," screeched Courtney,"I can't believe you got on stage!" In reality, neither could Marta.

"What did he say to you up there?" Katrina chimed in.

"That if I ever need a favor," said Marta grasping the autographed photo, "he would be there for me." she dreamily replied in a daze.

"Oh, brother!" laughed Katrina as the girls sat back in their seats to listen to the next song.

"OK ladies and gentlemen, thank you for being such a great audience tonight. Now we're going to slow things down with this little number we call 'There Was a Miracle'. He grabbed his acoustic guitar from the stand next to the microphone, put the strap over his shoulder, and began to play the enchanting, melodic guitar intro and sing,

"There was a miracle, there was a miracle. And it happened just like that, just like that..."

The girls swayed back and forth to the comforting melody, still on a cloud from Marta meeting Slate when *the phone rang!*

This ear piercing noise shocked Marta right out of her memory, and back to present day, in her room, at her desk, with the considerable stresses she had to face.

She lowered one side of her headphones to eavesdrop on the phone call, though she could only hear one side of it. Grandpa Rogelio's side of it.

"Yes, hello? Yes, yes. Well, no we do not have the payment, but- Well, yes of course! But- we need more time to- Yes, I understand. Ok, thank you. Please do what you can, do what you can."

She heard the phone loudly clang back onto the base.

"What did the banker say?" asked Lupita, Marta's grandmother.

"That we have to come up with $5,700 by the fifteenth, or we will lose Leon Picante."

The small mom-and-pop authentic Latino cuisine restaurant had been in the family for over 40 years. It was the lifeblood of the Leon family, and the first business her grandparents established when they moved to the United States from Puerto Juan, a tiny island in the Caribbean.

"But what about the federal assistance programs?" Lupita asked.

"The SBA ran out of money, and we would not have qualified anyway."

Marta was still listening, and knew that even though *she* was a citizen, her grandparents were not, and that is why they would not qualify for help from the government.

"Why should our immigration status matter? We have been paying taxes in this country for 38 years. They never question our status when they are accepting our money." Lupita huffed.

"I know, mi amor," Rogelio said as he put his strong arm around his wife, "but the money is due, and we are all out of options. It would take a miracle for this all to work out" He looked uncharacteristically defeated, but tried to hide his fear from his wife.

"Well then, my husband, un milagro sera! A miracle will come. Hay que mantener la fey. We have got to keep the faith." Lupita was scared too, but her faith in God was stronger. It held the family together in tough times, and she knew she would have to stay strong and trust that God would come through for them once again.

Marta put her headphones all the way back on, and made sure not to let the floor squeak as she readjusted herself in her computer chair. She hit play on her music player and heard, "-with love, love, love, love, love, love, love!" and thought to herself,

"a miracle...what about Slate?".

Thoughts and ideas flooded her mind as the plan suddenly came to her of how she could help save the restaurant. She remembered the promise he made to her on stage at that concert two years ago. She remembered that he said if she ever needed a favor, that he would be there for her. She opened the top drawer of her desk and took out her stationary. The first card on top had a bright pattern, with stripes and splotches, and a red envelope to go with it. She opened the card, and began to write:

"*Dear Slate,*

My name is Marta Ramona Leon, and I live in Tafticopa, CA. 2 years ago, you lost your bracelet at a concert in Bakersfield, and I was the girl that gave it back to you. You gave me an autograph, and told me that if I ever needed a favor, that you would be there for me. I think I need that favor now. The pandemic and lockdowns have lasted so long that my grandparents' restaurant, Leon Picante is close to going out of business. We have to raise $5,700 by the 15th or else, my family and me, we lose everything. I want to throw a benefit concert to raise the money. You are my very favorite rock star, and I need a headliner for the show. People will come to the concert if they know you will be performing. I really need a miracle, and I know you might be busy, but I pray that you can come through. If you can, the concert is going to be at 5:30 pm at the Tafticopa Memorial Park in Tafticopa, CA. Thank you for reading my letter. I do hope you will come.

With Sincerest Hope,
Your Fan Marta"

She folded the letter, put it in the red envelope, wrote "To Slate" and the address listed on the back of the 'Growing Pains in Willowmore' album on the outside, and gripped it to her chest. She said a prayer to herself with her eyes closed while holding the letter tightly.

"Dear God. We need a miracle. I believe. I have faith. I pray you will be there for me and my family. Please let this letter get there in time." After praying over it, she put the letter next to the other packages she had to take to the post office, and put a big Overnight Delivery stamp on it.

She felt a little better, but knew she had a lot of work to do. She reached for her phone and found Katrina and Courtney's emojis in her call log. She pushed both circles at once, and started a three-way video chat.

"Got your S.O.S", said Courney. "What's going on?"

"Same," chimed in Katrina, "This better be a real emergency."

"Meet me at the park behind Leon Picante, tomorrow, at noon." Marta smiled at her two best friends who both knew she had something up her sleeve.

"Oh brother!" said Katrina as she rolled her eyes.

"We will be there for sure." said Courtney in her typical chipper fashion.

The girls all got off of the call, and Marta got back on her computer to start planning out the details, and setting up the web page for the concert. As she created the social media page, 'Leon Picante Benefit Concert', she wondered to herself if this could really work. She spent the rest of the afternoon, and evening planning out the details in her head, and setting up the Pay Q App on her phone before getting tired and moseying over to her bed. She had so many pillows on her bed that she had to move some of them to the side, not to mention Mr. Tompkins, her 25 pound fluffy tabby cat, just so she could have room to lay down. As soon as her head touched the pillow, she knocked out in an exhausted slumber.

CHAPTER 2

The Legacy

The next morning she was woken up by Mr. Tompkins massage-scratching her back to get her attention. She rolled over and patted him on the head.

"It's a little early, kitty, but I guess I needed to get up early anyway."

Marta was responsible for doing prep at Leon Picante. She had to cut all of the vegetables, and pre-season the meat for the day, not to mention set the tables, and write the dish of the day in marker on the big whiteboard. Those were her duties, and she had done them since she started high school. She got out of bed, brushed her teeth, put on her shorts and blouse, and headed out the door. Grandma Lupita needed all the help she could get since she had to lay off most of the workers during the pandemic.

She hopped in her truck and buckled her seatbelt. It was an old beat up truck, but she bought it herself with money she earned working for her grandparents and babysitting on the side. Nothing fancy, but it had a CD player and Bluetooth capabilities, and took her everywhere she needed to go. Even if it was just a few blocks down the street and around the corner.

'Flautas Con Salsa Picante' she wrote after she arrived at Leon Picante when she had finished cutting the vegetables, seasoning the meat, and setting the tables.

"Grandma, why does every dish seem to come with Salsa Picante?" She asked her grandmother who was stirring some soup in a big pot in the kitchen."

Grandma Lupita looked up from the pot and said, "Oh my dear, it does not only seem that way, it is that way! Every dish does come with my World Famous Salsa Picante. It was passed down from my great grandmother, to my grandmother, to my mother, to-"

Marta cut her off before she could finish, "My grandmother!"

Lupita giggled and replied, "Yes, mi hijita. To me, and now to you. Come over here and stir this for me while I get out the book, and finally tell you the recipe. I think you are ready, and there has never been a better time."

Marta began to walk over, when the alarm on her phone went off saying that it was 5 minutes to noon. "Oh Abuela, I would love to, but I have to take a raincheck! I am meeting the girls at Centennial Memorial Park and if I don't leave right now, I am going to be late."

Grandma Lupita continued stirring the soup, and added a sprinkle of cilantro before saying, "Ok, mi hijita. Say hi to Katrina and Courtney for me, and make sure to call me if you are going to be out later than dark"

"Yes Abuela, I will. Oh, and the chile verdes and onions are already cut and separated. See you this evening, Grandma." It kind of annoyed her that Grandma Lupita still babied her, but the older she got, the more she appreciated the concern. She grabbed her bag as she rushed out the door, making the bell attached to the door frame jingle like a christmas bell.

"Goodbye, my beautiful granddaughter. May God bless you with protection and love in your adventures." Lupita continued stirring the soup with a peaceful grin on her face. She knew they would hardly get any customers that day, the same as every other day since the restrictions were slightly eased, but something about stirring the soup gave her a nice calm.

Marta was on the run, making sure she could get to the park on time. This was not too hard to do considering the park was only a block away on the street behind the restaurant. Tafticopa was a small town with a population of only about 2,700 to 2,703 people, depending on what year of the census you were reading. Old buildings and storefronts made out of brick from the early 1900s lined North St. in the historic business district.

Tafticopa had fallen on some tough economic times, even before the pandemic, and many of the storefronts were empty, but it was still the kind of place you would want to raise your family. Good schools, a community center, a lot of churches and restaurants, and a community college that had the best baseball team in the region. Movies at the historic Fox Theatre on friday nights, and parks and trails that snaked for miles throughout the town, and even into the deserty hills. Oil and agriculture were the two main industries, and the culture was half English speaking, half Spanish speaking, and part *Spanglish* speaking, if that math could even add up. Marta probably fit into the Spanglish category, though she was raised by her grandparents who spoke English well, but Spanish as their first language.

She pulled up in her old clunker and parked right next to Courtney's Jeep, and Katrina's Honda. Courtney had the nicest car by far, but her dad did pretty much buy it for her. Katrina got her mom's old car when she upgraded to a Bimmer last year.

Just as her watch turned to 12 o'clock, Marta spotted the girls sitting in the grass under the tree they all loved. That was their spot, and she knew just where they would be. Even though the girls were sitting far apart trying to socially distance,

Courtney still wore her mask. She had asthma which made her immunocompromised so she had to be extra careful during the pandemic. Her mask matched her bright pink flowered shirt, so she could still be fashion forward while being safe.

Katrina was in her typical black slightly emo looking clothes. She liked to accessorize, but it was mostly with chokers and spikey chain bracelets. She used to be a bit more bubbly, but started only wearing black after her parents got divorced and her dad moved away.

Marta pulled her blanket out of her bag and set it 6ft from the other girls so that they could sit in a big spaced out triangle. They sort of looked like hippies in a meadow for the 1960's. When they settled down after greeting each other, Marta began to tell them the plan.

"So that's the bottom line. Either my grandparents and me raise $5,700 in 3 days, or they lose the restaurant, and we lose everything."

"Where would you live?", asked Courtney.

"Probably have to move back to Puerto Juan with my great, great great...I don't know...aunt, or worse, Alaska with my mom. I mean, I love my Alaskan side, and I'm down with the Iditarod, but I don't ever want to eat that much elk again.", replied Marta.

"Alaska. Meh. Ugh. Gives me the skeevies!" said Katrina in her melancholy way.

"Exactly." said Marta.

"So let me get this straight. You want to have a concert, during this pandemic, to raise $5 thousand dollars, in like...3 days?" asked Katrina raising her eyebrow.

Marta nodded and replied, "Yup. Or else...skeevies."

"Well we can't have that. You are our best friend. I don't want you to be that far. I don't want you to freeze! How do we pull this off?" asked a concerned Courtney.

Marta smiled and looked each one of them in their eyes.

"Katrina, I need you to ask your mom if we can borrow that lot you guys own with that old sign on it. We gotta make this an outdoor concert, and the sign will get even more people to buy tickets."

"Fine, whatever." said Katrina nonchalantly.

"Courtney, I need you to ask your dad if we can borrow speakers and lights from his music store." said Marta.

" The Sound Shop is pretty much shut down because of the pandemic so I'm sure he would let us."

"Ya just tell him it's for a college project, and you need it to get an A. He always comes through for school stuff. If it's for school, he's cool." Katrina rhymed.

At this moment, Marta stood up, and with the conviction of a charismatic preacher, or maybe a drill sergeant, she ordered, "Move out, ladies! We've got a lot of work to do."

She began to roll up her blanket and put it back in her bag to leave and get started on all they had to do when Katrina spoke up and asked, "Wait princess, what are you bringing to the table?"

Marta put her blanket in her bag, zipped up the zipper, and looked directly at the girls. "Why, the talent of course. Girl Power!"

The girls looked at each other puzzled as Marta trotted off giddily skipping and giggling down the walking path and back to her truck, excited that she was at least going to try to help her grandparents save the restaurant. Katrina and Courtney sat for a few more moments, then looked at each other and laughed too as they packed up their blankets, and went separate ways to their cars and homes.

CHAPTER 3

Katrina and Courtney

Marta was so excited to get things rolling that she had already printed up fliers and tickets to take with her throughout the neighborhood. She had already done her summer school assignments the night before so she would have all day to go canvassing and knock on doors.

She drove to The Heights, a neighborhood in one of the nicest parts of town, hoping that the people there would have money to support, or at least take some pity on her and the situation. The people that answered could either buy a ticket right then for $10, or use the contactless Pay Q App Marta installed on her phone. She started in the neighborhood near the park and went from door to door.

"Would you like to buy a ticket to a Slate and The Muggy Hamsters Concert for this Friday at 5:30pm to help support Leon Picante?" she would ask over and over again. Most people politely declined.

She met several odd and quirky characters that would give her answers ranging from, "Sure, I would love to buy a ticket and attend", to, "Oh I'm sorry, I can't go. I am socially distancing because of the pandemic," to strange responses like "Sorry, I will be busy that night cleaning my mirrors while watching the meteor shower, but here's a donation!" and the even stranger, "I can't. I don't want to, and anyway, I am washing my brother in law's cat that night. Meow."

Some people, mostly the artists, did buy a ticket though. Jerri Love, one of the sweetest and most beautiful girls in town bought two tickets, and even offered to perform ballet at the event. Maybe she could get other dancers and performers to want to help too.

Toby Applebox said maybe the other loaders at the grocery store would come.

Most of the people were supportive, at least in their encouragement, but some were just plain odd, and Marta was happy she wore her mask, especially when someone would cough a little or sneeze.

While Marta was working away on day one of selling tickets and putting the word out about the concert, her best friends were at their houses trying to get their parents to help them out with what Marta had asked for. The concert was a bit of a secret, because all of the parents knew each other pretty well, and the girls did not want Grandma Lupita and Grandpa Rogelio to find out about the concert, and be disappointed if they did not raise enough money. They also did not want them to feel any shame for needing the help.

Courtney was up first. Her dad was home from work early that day. He was closing up the shop in the early afternoon since the pandemic started because he simply was not selling and renting enough equipment throughout the days to keep the pre-pandemic hours. He did not seem to mind the extra down time, and Courtney caught him just as he was fussing at his favorite basketball team for missing a free throw on a rerun of the NBA finals he taped from 8 years ago. "Make the basket! You guys get paid millions of dollars every year to make the best plays possible and you give the game away by missing a free throw. Come on!" He was fussing at the players on the TV, but he was not really in a bad mood. He just liked to yell at the TV sometimes, and shouting at the players made him feel like part of the action.

"Hi Daddy!", Courtney popped in front of the TV and said.

"Oh Hi, honey. How is summer school going?"

"It's going great Daddy." Courtney was a bit of a Daddy's girl. Her mom had passed away when she was very young, so it was just her and her dad from as far back as she could remember. She was super girly, but also loved watching sports with her dad, and could easily spot the difference between a layup and a hook shot.

"In fact, I have a group project due in my Music Appreciation class, and I need speakers and lights for the presentation. Could I borrow some from the shop?"

Her dad, Conrad Croutonberg quickly replied, "Sure thing, Kiddo! The Yakazumos put out the best sound, but the Haraties have the best tone. Why don't you take them both. Oh, and the lights are in the back room."

"Thank you Daddy!" she exclaimed as she hugged him and ran out of the room.

As she left, Mr. Crountonberg thought to himself, "Hmmm, I have never heard of needing lights for a music appreciation class." He looked confused for a moment, but then shrugged and said, "Oh, well. Times sure have changed." as he hit the play button to pick up the game where he paused it. Courtney was already in her white jeep convertible, halfway down the street, and on the way to the shop to pick up the equipment.

Katrina's Mom Kimberly worked in the business district near the park. She ran a real estate company, and managed rental units and vacant storage lots for machinery and trailers. She was the CEO, and always on *very* important phone calls.

"No, Fred. That is not how we do it. You always bill the supplier first, and then average the interest! Fix it, and get back to me ASAP!"

She was just hanging up the phone with the employee when Katrina burst in the room and blurted, "Mom, is the East Lot empty, and can I use it?"

Mrs. Kobaldini did not even look up from the paperwork she was reviewing and replied, "Well yes it is technically vacant. Actually, the county made us move everyone to the northern lot because of social distancing. But I don't...", Katrina cut her off before she could say no.

"Mom, I just really wanted to do some interpretive dancing to...express myself. The only place big enough to do my...art...is the East Lot." She said this while doing a funky yoga-looking dance, and waving her arms around like a flamingo.

"Express yourself?" Her mom was suspicious and finally looked up while Katrina was wrapping up her flappy dance demonstration. She suspiciously asked, "Oh really?" and then said, "Ok. Well, I would not want to get in the way of you 'expressing' yourself...You can use the lot..."

"And the sign?" Katrina hastily squeezed in.

"Ya Katrina, but only until things open back up and I need it again. We get half of our revenue from that lot and-"

Before her mom could change her mind, Katrina blurted out, "Thanks mom!" She gleefully walked behind her mom's big corner desk, and they shared a rare hug. Katrina was normally not a hugger, at all. Strange. She then hurried out of the office before her mom could change her mind.

As the door closed behind her, Mrs. Kobaldini realized to herself, "Wait, the sign? Why on Earth does she need the sign?"

She stood up as if to go after Katrina, and called out..." Katrina!" after her, but it was too late. Katrina had already left the building.

CHAPTER 4

Lupita, Rogelio, and Federica

Early the next day, all of the girls were already out covering the different neighborhoods. Sometimes they stuck together, and other times they split up and each tackled a street of their own. They got a lot of weird responses, and even more rejections, but a fair number of people were indeed buying tickets. Slate was a pretty popular artist amongst the young adults and teens, and he had gotten even more popular when his music made it to the mainstream radio stations and he started his Trans-TransAtlantic World Tour.

Leon Picante was always closed on Thursdays. Ever since it opened in the 1970s, Marta's Grandparents had taken every Thursday off to rest, and have couple's time. Grandma Lupita always said that it kept their marriage feeling as fresh as a spring flower, and by the looks of it, she was right. Sometimes they would spend the day having a nice picnic in the orchards, or holding hands walking down Main Street to catch a movie, and other times they would take out Grandpa Rogelio's 1964 classic Ford Mustang Convertible for a ride to the coast. This was the first car he bought when they arrived to the United States, and he had kept it ever since. He even named her Frederica because she was such a looker. Frederica had a special place in the garage, and Grandpa Rogelio's heart. On that day, she was the chariot that would take them to their favorite cliffside parking spot to watch the boats come and go in the harbor below them, and ease the tension and stress they were feeling.

They had to take a route through the mountains, even though Tafticopa was nicknamed 'The Key to the Sea'. It got that moniker because it was the only route to the ocean for that part of Central California, unless you wanted to drive down to So Cal or up and to the West. Really, Tafticopa was a fork in the road, and a truckstop, as it was the only gas station around for miles, but the forced stop meant that a diverse stream of people flowed through the town, especially on the weekends as people from Bakersfield, Fresno, Tehachapi, San Francisco and beyond trickled through the small town pitstop.

Rogelio and Lupita drove the windy two lane road through Los Padres National Forest that cloudy day. It took them a few hours to arrive, but they were not in any rush. They even stopped at an avocado, honey, and mango stand along the side of the road to get some fresh locally grown produce in Ojai. These day trips were magical for the two, and getting away from the city, even a small town like Tafticopa reminded them of the simpler time and place that they came from.

They drove with the top down on Frederica, and the wind in their hair. They drove through passages lined with huge old trees that seemed to hold hands with each other from each side over the road. This was one of their favorite parts of the familiar ride because the trees created a sort of tunnel. One could even call it a tunnel of love. When they finally arrived at their secret parking spot, after driving through the beautiful cloudy mountains on roads with no guard rails, they got out of the car and leaned back on the bumper. This spot was their favorite because to the unskilled eye, it just looked like a dense, impenetrable forest from the road, but for those who ventured down the path, the trees opened up to a beautiful clearing with a bird's eye view of the ocean and bay below. They held hands silently as they took in the view.

Lupita finally broke the silence. "Look at all the pretty ships, Mi Amor. Look at the waves. What a peace they bring."

"I used to think so. They remind me of the fishing boats in baja.", Rogelio replied.

"Ah. Yes, Mi Amor. Baja. You looked so cute scaling the salmon as they came in.", she remembered.

Rogelio softened his stance as the memory and responded, "And you looked so hot and spicy fileting them." He pulled her closer playfully, passionately and they were then facing each other.

"We worked so hard to get from the shipyard," Lupita remembered, contemplating life in the old country.

"Yes, to selling my World Famous Salsa Picante in Puerto Juan.

Lupita playfully put a scowl on her face and asked, "Your World Famous Salsa Picante? How can that be when it was passed down to me by my grandmother? So machismo, taking credit where it is not due."

They both laughed as this was a familiar debate they liked to have with each other. The laughter faded when Rogelio remembered the financial predicament they were in.

"Well, I could use a line of credit right now. I just can't believe that we will lose the restaurant if we don't come up with the money. This is ridiculous. It is not our fault that the economy was shut down for so long. I mean, we rode out the Recession of 2008 but this?"

His expression changed as he recalled more details about life in Puerto Juan. "I loved the shipyard because there, I found you, but that was all I found. 3 nickels a pop for all that hard work, being too brown even for that country...I don't ever want to go back to struggling like that again."

Lupita could sense that her husband was giving up hope, and was beyond worried about Leon Picante. She spun to face him and looked directly into his emotional dark eyes.

"Rogelio, when we were almost blocked from getting our visas, did God make a way?"

He nodded, "Yes, Lupita."

She added, "When we thought we would not be able to get your medicine due to the Great Shortage, did God make a way?"

"Si, Mi Amor.", he quickly responded.

"And when I thought all hope was lost for us to have a child of our own, did God not bless us with the most amazing son?

They both paused after that question and watched a sailboat pull out of its docking position and start to make its way down the passage in the bay toward the open sea. Memories flooded their minds as visions of Raul came sharply into focus.

Lupita had visions of throwing a football back and forth with her young son in the front yard at night, lit only by the porch light. It was she that taught him how to put just enough spin on the ball to get it to spiral.

Rogelio remembered whittling away at a rectangle of wood, and turning it into a race car with his son to be launched for the Pinewood Car Race for the Woodland Scouts. He remembered the smile on Raul's face after they added the weights to the front, and watched it speed past the competition in the final round. First place.

Lupita also remembered the day Raul left to go to Westpoint, the military academy. He looked so proud standing on the stairs, suitcase in hand, and that Westpoint Cap on his head. His beard had just started to fill in and darken, and she knew her son was now a man. She remembered straightening his collar, and giving him a hug while praying that he would always come back home safely.

Raul completed his studies at Westpoint, married an ambitious young writer, and had two daughters. Marta, and her older sister Adriana. They were a happy little family, even though Marta was just a baby. When the United States was attacked on September 11th, 2001, Raul's squadron was deployed. He was a captain in the Army after studying at Westpoint and completing Officer Candidate School. He was a forward observer which meant that he was responsible for going before his comrades and calling in the heavy artillery over his head to strike enemy targets in front of him, and clear the way for the rest of the soldiers. On a dark Friday night, while calculating coordinates to call in the target, a sniper spotted him, shot one time, and killed him. Shot through the heart.

When the military drove up to their house, and knocked on the door, Lupita's heart sank when she saw the uniformed men. In her heart she knew that her baby was gone, for her's fluttered and stalled days earlier as she washed dishes in the kitchen. Her motherly intuition was correct. They buried him the next week, a hero's ceremony with a 21 gun salute, and Rogelio was never the same.

Neither was Raul's wife Ruth, Marta and Adriana's mother. She moved to the most isolated part of Alaska she could find after dropping both of the tiny girls off with their grandparents to be raised. Her grief never subsided, though she channeled it into her writing and became a poet.

Adriana was almost 4 years old at the time, while Marta was just a baby. Marta never really knew her father, though she had his deep set eyes. Adriana took after her mother, and as soon as she graduated high school, left Tafticopa for the big city. She wanted to get a good education, but also wanted to leave behind the sad memories she never healed from and start a new life. She was only semi-successful in doing so because she called just about every day to check on everyone in the family, and always had a bit of a pessimistic chip on her shoulder she could not shake. She had been through too much, at too young of an age, but she did try to make the best of her circumstances.

When a gust of wind brushed past Lupita's face back on the cliff, she remembered that Raul had told her that God would always be with her, and if he did not come home, to have the faith to know he was with the Lord. She could process this, and used these memories as a source of her strength. It helped her to keep her faith in God strong. It comforted her and gave her purpose. Rogelio struggled longer with it. She could see in his eyes that he was in the empty place he sometimes drifted too when reminded of uncomfortable truths.

After Lupita stared at her husband with a gaze of concern, Rogelio finally responded and said, "Yes, though he took him away 28 years later for someone else's war."

Lupita did not want him to slip into a depression, not with all that they were facing with the potential closing of the restaurant, and the changes that would bring. She straightened her back and lifted her chin up.

"The important thing is not what was lost, but simply what was. We wouldn't have such wonderful granddaughters to raise if the circumstances were not just so. Adriana is the first girl in our family to go away to college. And Marta...She is beautiful. She is strong. Our future does not lie in the bones of a restaurant, so easily swept away by the waves, but in the heart of our family. God has never failed us. He will not start today."

Lupita said this to her husband in a moment of strength and compassion. They shared a tender moment followed by a close eyed kiss as the ocean breeze danced around them.

This got his attention and snapped him out of his sadness, but only long enough to remember the issue they were still facing. "But the bill is due, and I don't have a backup plan this time."

"Well, you could always sell the mustang", Lupita joked.

"Frederica? My baby? No way. Surely you jest!" Rogelio Laughed. "She's the only other woman who has ever captured my heart. Plus, KBB on her is only about $2,070. I already looked into it."

They both laughed at the irony of their predicament.

"Well then, you really better start praying for a miracle, Buddy, and believing it will come."

They were still pleasant and enjoying their special time together, after all, this was their favorite secret spot, on a Thursday, and they were in love. But the reality of losing Leon Picante weighed heavy on them as the sun began to set and they watched the boats begin to dock.

"Yes, Mi Amor", he whispered, "a miracle".

They held each other until the sun set, then got back inside Frederica, and began their windy journey back home.

CHAPTER 5

Unglued

Marta and the girls had been knocking on doors in the neighborhood for hours. They sold a decent amount of tickets, but not nearly enough to save the restaurant. The girls all met up at the park like they discussed just as the sun was setting. Courtney hugged them both, and then took off.

"My Dad is still a stickler for me getting back home when the street lights come on. I gotta call it a night."

She hugged both of them, and they watched for safety as she walked across the grass down the walking path to her Jeep and took off.

Marta turned to Katrina who was checking her watch as if to say she was ready to turn in too. Katrina yawned a big long yawn, and said "Well, I guess we better call it a night too. I don't think we are going to sell any more tickets tonight."

"Great! Are you quitting on me too? I guess nobody wants to help me. Nobody cares!", Marta snarled.

"Quitting? Are you serious? I, we, have all put everything on hold to help you sell tickets for this stupid concert that is magically supposed to keep your grandparents' restaurant from closing. This is the thanks for walking around in this heat all day, and faking a smile, talking to strangers and begging them to help?"

"If you don't want to help me then just go!"

Katrina was not going to let Marta off the hook that easily. They had been friends long enough to know how to have the tough talks and get to the bottom of their issues.

"Marta, I think we both know I would have rather spent my day playing video games and sleeping, but I am here. You believe this is going to work. Well, I, we believe in you. Courtney does too. We love you and we are here for you. I'm just saying, the concert...is kind of a long shot, and anyway, if we are going to pull it off tomorrow, we both need to get some sleep. You look awful."

Marta looked at Katrina, and then looked down at herself. Her shirt was half untucked and had a coffee stain right down the middle from when she canvassed in the Business District and the owner of Opal Mary's Coffee Shack gave her one on the house. She would have rather she bought a ticket, or 10, but was thankful for the coffee. It was actually all she ate that day. Ok, she did look a bit worn out.

"Fine. Ok, Katrina you are right. I'm tired too, and I'm sorry. I love you guys. Thank you so much for helping me." Marta acquiesced as she gave Katrina a hug.

"Best friends for life, Marta"

"Yes, best friends for life".

They both walked together to their cars. Tafticopa was a beautiful small town, but its quaintness did attract the odd drifter, and some people that were addicted to drugs. They both watched each other get into their cars and start the engines. They waved as Katrina pulled off.

Marta just sat in her truck for a moment and let the gravity of the circumstances set in. She was processing. The concert was the next day, and they had to put the rest of their hope into people buying enough tickets at the gate to make up the missing money, or in the remote possibility that Slate and the band would show up and somehow save the day. Marta was not even sure if Slate had received the letter, and if Overnight Delivery was even still a guarantee during the pandemic. She was exhausted, spiritually, physically, and emotionally. It did not help that she had a nagging older sister that would video message her all the time and point out everything that could go wrong. Just then, like clockwork, her phone rang and of course, it was Adriana. She was not feeling up to taking the call that night, but against her better judgment, took it anyway as she sat under the streetlight with her truck running.

CHAPTER 6

Adriana and Fozzy

"I got your email about the plan to save Leon Picante, Marta. This is stupid. You might as well start packing, and get used to elk burgers and snow boots. Why would Slate come play a concert in Tafticopa?"

"I already told you. I sent him a letter asking if he can help us save Leon Picante and perform at the concert. Slate said if I ever needed a favor to hit him up. This...is a favor." Marta responded to her older sister.

Adriana was in her dorm finishing up a submission to grad school, and Marta checked the Pay Q App on her phone one more time to see if anyone else was interested in attending the concert or donating. Nobody. She then put the truck into gear, and headed towards home.

"That was like 2 years ago! He is probably somewhere in Italy right now, or Africa. Isn't he on his TRANS-TRANSATLANTIC TOUR? He's a bonafide Trans Pop Star now. Way too busy for un concierto in little old Tafticopa."

She was right about that. Slate and The Muggy Hamsters had grown a lot in popularity in the 2 years since that concert. Slate was a man of trans experience, and finally let the world know after being scared it would ruin his career. It did the opposite, and he became a sensation that even more people fell in love with because he was living his truth. It didn't really matter to Marta or the other girls. Slate was Slate, and he was still just as dreamy as ever. Only now he was a bit harder to keep track of because he was off performing all around the world, from Tokyo to Timbuktu.

"Well it doesn't hurt to try. I don't see you coming up with a better plan, and our grandparents freaking need us. We can't let them lose the restaurant." Marta said matter of factly as she turned the corner, and onto her street.

"Leon Picante has been in the family for over 40 years. They love it. They got married there. What are you going to do if Mr. Slate doesn't show up." said Adriana, always looking for a worst case scenario.

"He's gonna show", said Marta as she pulled into the driveway and put the truck in park, "I know he will."

"And if he doesn't?" pushed Adriana.

Why did she have to be that way, thought Marta, but deep down she knew it was just how Adriana had become. They didn't get to see their mom very often which was a bigger deal for Adriana, because she was old enough to remember what life was like when her family was all together. She had to grow up faster than Marta which made her mind always look for possible threats. She was not totally wrong in her approach, because sometimes things did go wrong, but Marta was simply not in the mood for an Adriana funk-fest tonight.

"Dang Debby Downer," she replied, "If he doesn't show then we just sell as many tickets as we can and I will get Fozzy down the street to perform. He has been wanting to be a DJ since like 8th grade. In fact, maybe I will ask him tomorrow."

Marta looked down at Adriana's face on the video messenger, and Adriana's eyes got huge at the memory.

"Ew gross." she said, "Don't you remember what happened when I asked him for help at the Bake Sale last year?"

Of course Marta remembered. Everyone did. How could they not, Adriana was the type of girl who wouldn't let you forget something like that.

"Yes, I remember". Marta sighed as she already knew this story, and that Adriana would make sure to tell it to her again.

"It was a few days before the Church Bake Sale that I was in charge of organizing." Adriana began, seemingly whisked back in time as she told the story.

"Fozzy had signed up to volunteer and man the cake walk station, but every time I called him to narrow down the details, I got his stupid voicemail.

> 'Hi this is Fozzy'" she mimicked his voice, "'if you got my voicemail, I'm off catching some waves. Leave a message and I might get back to you...if you are lucky.'

"How obnoxious! Anyway I happened to see him when I was walking through the park and he was just leaning against the bike racks with his skateboard, listening to music as if he had absolutely nothing to do. I walked right up to him and said 'Hey! You never got back to me. Can you please help out at the bake sale on Friday?' He acted like this was brand new information, as if he hadn't signed up to volunteer his time and said,

'Um, ok sure. That sounds great. How much does it pay?' I could not believe he was asking me that. 'Hello...nothing!' I told him, 'This is a benefit bake sale, Fozzy!' and he was like, 'Well I was just trying to see what the benefit is to me. Maybe you can give me a kiss, and I will take you out for a Sno-White Ice Cream Cone.' and he actually closed his eyes and leaned in smacking his gross lips, trying to kiss me. I, of course, ducked like a ninja and dodged it just in time.

By this point in the story Marta's mind had already been drifting to wondering how many people would show up, and if they would raise enough money to pay the bank, and how much she would hate it if she had to eat elk at her mom's house in Alaska. Plus, everyone knew that Adriana secretly liked the attention she got from Fozzy, and from telling that story over and over. If Fozzy wasn't a year younger than her, she probably would have been up to dating him. After all he did grow up right down the street, but she had a thing against May September relationships, and blocked the whole scenario before it ever had a chance.

"I screamed and told him, 'Ew Fozzy you effing know better. Just show up for the bake sale, bring some brownies, and don't be late.' I walked away and left him standing there with that goofy puppy dog look on his face. I made sure to swish when I walked so he could have the memory of me stuck in his mind since he wanted to kiss me so bad."

"Right. Right" said Marta as she started to get out of the truck, "But we need as much help as we can get."

"Okay. Okay. Ask him, but if he flirts with you...I just hope you have some pepper spray..!" said Adriana right as Lupita crept up to the truck in her nightgown to check on Marta. They had just gotten home a little earlier, but Marta did not even notice that Frederica was in the driveway.

Grandma Lupita charged right up to door and fussed,

"Who's going to flirt with my granddaughter? Whose butt do I have to kick? I will pour some of my famous salsa on him if he-" Before she could finish her sentence, Marta had already hung up the video call, and got out of the truck to greet her.

"-It's nobody, abuela!" she said as she leaned in and tightly hugged Grandma Lupita who had a kind soft smile on by that point.

"Believe me, you have nothing to worry about, Grandma. You have nothing to worry about." said Marta as they hung on to each other tight in an embrace. Grandma Lupita knew that she had nothing to worry about in the boys department. Marta had a few boyfriends throughout the years, but nothing had ever gotten too serious. Marta was more focused on achieving goals than finding Mr. Right, at least at that time. She was specifically worried about saving the restaurant, and tried to be strong for her grandma who she knew was definitely worried too. They hugged for a bit longer, before letting go, and they walked in the house together to get ready for bed.

By the time she stopped by the kitchen and grabbed a leftover tamal, and headed down the hall to her room, Marta was about ready to lay down, and kicked off her sneakers to climb into bed. She knew she would not be able to sleep through the whole night, because so much was rushing through her head and there was still so much to do, but her body was tired and needed to lay down for at least a little while. She scrolled through posts on social media looking for any signs of donations, or a random magical message from Slate, and fell asleep to a church service playing softly on the living room TV in the distance. Gloria Hallelujah was singing a hymn while Pastor Antonio delivered the sermon. Grandma Lupita always left the TV playing the Faith and Works Channel to listen to the rebroadcast of First

Congressional's weekly service. The familiarity soothed the household.

"You have to have faith, for it is faith that enables God to work a miracle...*un milagro* in every situation in your life. Trust in The Lord with all your soul, and with all your mind, and with all your heart, and watch your blessings unfold before you. For The Lord is faithful to His people, and He wants to bless you. He wants to save you. Jesus loves each and every one of you. Leave it at the cross, and at the feet of The Most High. God bless you. Good Night."

CHAPTER 7

The Muggy Hamsters

12:02am at a dingy little diner on old Route 66 in Palm Springs. A waitress with grey curly hair and a striped pink apron walked over with plates stacked all the way up her arm, and set down three meals. Ham, cheddar eggs, and toast on the right, cottage cheese, fruit and a whole wheat bagel in the middle, and waffles so big they hung off the plate on the left. The waffles were decadently covered in fresh picked strawberries, served with two eggs and bacon, and had a ball of whipped cream on top that was so big, it looked like a cloud.

"Thanks" said Scarlet, who was scooched in next to Davey in the cracked comfortable ruby booth. Slate had not arrived yet, but these were The Muggy Hamsters who had just played a show with him at the Casino Montreal Rensuke, and were absolutely starving for some breakfast food. Scarlet had ordered for Slate because she knew just how he liked his eggs; scrambled medium with sharp cheddar on top. They began to dig in.

"Do you think they have real whipped cream here or the fake stuff?", asked Davey as he cut another piece of the waffle and began piling on the toppings.

"Davey, what's the difference? Cream is cream. You're gonna spread it on your little waffles and scarf them down in like 5 minutes anyway. Does it really matter?", said Scarlet in her sassy way.

"Oh it matters, it *super* matters" said Davey with the huge piece in his mouth. Davey was a little older than the other members of the band. He was the replacement for the original drummer, Timpani Sticks, who left the group just before they got big to join the Chicago Philharmonic when her cousin got her an audition to be first chair.

Davey liked to eat, didn't like to bathe, and only had a cul de sac of hair with a few wispy strands on top, but man, could he play. He got his start playing in a ska band in the 1990s and had a quality to his playing that fit right in with The Muggy Hamsters.

"Super!" said Scarlet sarcastically with a huge smile and a big thumbs up. Scarlet had dark hair, and beautiful slanted eyes. She always kept a few strands of her hair colored fire engine red. She had the kind of smile that could light up the whole room, but always switched it to a playful pout before anyone could notice. Her fishnets and jumbo boots made her look taller and tougher than she was, but the rifts she played on her bass guitar lived up to the image.

The two were laughing at how goofy she looked teasing him, when Slate finally showed up carrying a huge white post office box filled with letters, and slammed it down in the middle of the table.

"We got fan mail", said Slate as he took his seat next to Scarlet. He quickly grabbed the carrier and pushed it to the edge of the table when Scarlet gave him a dirty look for plopping it down in the middle of their meal. He hardly even noticed the food she had ordered for him because he was focussed on a letter he was already reading from the top of the pile...*a red letter.*

He opened the letter and continued where he left off reading to himself. The two band mates were enjoying their food and blowing spit wads at each other in between bites. Scarlet got annoyed that Slate was so into whatever was written in the letter that he would barely look up, and she blew a spitwad right at the side of his head. It landed on one of his curls, wiggled, and then fell to the seat without him even noticing.

"What's that Mr. Skastar? Another letter from one of your adoring fans?" said Scarlet as she took a bite of her cantaloupe. She said it in a sing songy whiney way, but did not want to let on that it was really bothering her.

"Or one of our stalkers" chuckled Davey as he chomped another waffle.

The two laughed and continued eating, but Scarlet was still watching Slate's intensity as he read the letter out of the corner of her eye.

"So who's the *hottie* that's got your nose all in that book...er...in that letter this time, Mr. Cruddy? In the 5 years we dated, I never got that kind of...focus."

She moved closer, as Slate was still completely focussed on the letter, and snapped her fingers right in his face.

"Hello!...Earth to Mr. Rockstar. Anybody home?"

Slate finished reading the letter just at that moment, and winked at Scarlet as he tucked it into the inside pocket of his leather rose studded vest.

"Don't be jealous, Scarlet" he said, "This is just from a friend".

He made up for his lack of attention by romantically grabbing her hand, pulling her close, and kissing her softly on her lips. They weren't exactly still a couple, but they were meant for each other, and that was enough for them...for now.

"It better just be from a friend" said Scarlet as she relaxed into a grin and continued eating her food and making funny faces at Davey. Slate started eating his eggs too, but kept looking up to the ceiling with something clearly on his mind. The wheels were spinning, but he didn't want to be rude to his friends, so he cracked a quick joke that granted him entrance into their conversation, and let his rocker energy shine. It was a persona, but it was one that worked for him.

"Santa Maria was a tough crowd tonight", said Davey as he gulped down some milk.

Just then, the waitress came back, asked if everything was OK, and left them the bill. She shuffled back off toward the kitchen with her worn out shoes barely hanging on as the band chattered on about the gigs they had played, and what was still to come on this leg of their tour. The red letter stayed tucked in Slate's vest for the rest of the night, and they all stayed in that booth relaxing until the sun began to rise.

CHAPTER 8

The Recital

Marta was wide awake early that day, and sitting on the edge of her bed on her phone checking to see if any more last minute tickets were sold through the Pay Q App. Three. It was not enough.

Rogelio noticed her light was still on, knocked on her door, and went inside to check on her.

"Que tienes, chiquita? What's wrong?" He sat down on the bed and Marta finally broke down.

"I'm scared. I'm scared about what is going to happen if we lose Leon Picante. You guys worked so hard to build the business up. It seems like everything is going wrong and the walls are closing in on me. I want to help, and I am trying, but it all feels so much, and I am scared about what is going to happen."

He put his arm around her and she put her head on his shoulder while gripping a stuffed dragon her father had given her as a baby.

"Do you remember when you were in that ballet class, and you were too scared to go on stage for your recital?"

She nodded yes.

"Do you remember how you dressed me up in that tutu and tiara, and I danced along with you just off stage behind the curtain? You looked over at me and felt secure because you knew that no matter what, your Granpopop Rogelio would be there for you. I'm still here, Chiquita. Life can be scary at times, but you have to keep the faith. Everything is going to be OK, and I am not going anywhere. God is watching over us."

She needed that pep talk. The draining video calls with groaning Adriana, and the little spat between her and Katrina was enough to wipe her out. Rogelio stood up, kissed her on the forehead, and left the room. She plopped back on her pillow just for a moment, and stared up at the ceiling, and talked to God.

"Dear God, I know You are real. I know that You love us, and want to bless us. I am scared, but I am putting my faith in You, just like my Grandma Lupita and Grandpa Rogelio taught me. You can make a way out of no way, and I know You are very busy, but if You could please help me and my grandparents...we need You, Lord. Heavenly Father. Holy Spirit. Jesus. We need a miracle. I give it all to You. In Jesus name."

At the same time down the hall, in a closet sized room just for her, surrounded by tall burning saint and angel candles and incense, Grandma Lupita was praying too. The candles were the only light in the room and cast a heavenly glow, while the patchouli incense filled the space with an ethereal scent and smoke. Grandma Lupita was used to having to be strong for her family, but she was also used to leaning on God for all of her needs. In her long years, she had learned to trust Him for the big and the small, the insurmountable and the trivial. This was her way, and she got on her knees on a folded gold blanket, closed her eyes, and talked with God.

"Heavenly Father. In the name of your Holy Son Jesus, I come before You...I ask You". She hesitated, as her voice broke, "I need You. It is me, Lupita again Lord, and I am standing in the need of prayer. I come before You on behalf of my husband, and my family. As You know, the money is due for the restaurant, and our backs are up against the wall. I feel like we are out of options, and I don't know what else we can do. So I call on you

Lord God. Father, I give this situation to you. I cast my cares on You. I pray for a miracle to come through that You send straight from heaven. In Hebrews 13:5 You said 'Never will I leave you. Never will I forsake you.' So I am asking You to come through for us to help save our restaurant, our livelihood, Leon Picante. If You are willing, please help us. I pray this, Lord, yet not my will but Your will be done."

When she finished saying this, her eyes were still closed, and she gently folded her hands in her lap. She stayed like that for a few moments, meditating and regaining her strength as wisps from the incense danced through the air. She then stood up, placed the blanket on the back of the chair, and blew out all of the candles. All but one plain white one. She left that one lit as I sign of her hope, left the room and went off to prepare for the day. She caught a glimpse of Rogelio on his knees in meditation and prayer on the living room floor. She watched his back and shoulders move up and down as he breathed deeply in silent prayer. What miracle could God do to save them from this situation? She did not know, but somewhere deep within, she knew her prayers would be answered.

CHAPTER 9

The Community

The sun rose, and the dawn yielded to a blue sky day with clouds that looked painted onto a canvas. Marta, Courtney, and Katrina all met at the park, at noon, to get the event all set up. The concert was here. Fozzy and the Tafticopa Jazz Band had arrived with their own equipment, and were unloading their materials near the main stage across the grassy meadow behind the handball court. Saxophones, trumpets, trombones, drums, and a tuba, made their way to the stage. Courtney worked with Fozzy to connect the speakers and lights, while Katrina was painting finishing touches on signs that said, 'Tickets This Way', and 'Event Parking on First St.'. Everyone was finding their rhythm and the pieces seemed to be falling into place.

Marta was running from station to station making sure all of the elements were in order. A few of the other local businesses had booths set up to sell everything from flowers to burgers, while the Tafticopa Science Society had a popcorn booth where you could get a free scoop, and a packet of information on Sirius and the Epsilon Bootes star system. Marta's little neighbor Teresa and her brother and sister even had a lemonade stand. Even though it was just a table with some Dixie cups and a sign, the kids came ready with 2 wagons of lemons lined with American flags, a few boxes of sugar, and a huge construction site water buffalo tank their dad set up for them. They were ready to sell. Marta was their favorite babysitter, and they wanted to do everything in their young power to help her. Everyone was volunteering their products, their time, and all of their proceeds to try to help save Leon Picante, a gem in the community. The restaurant had a dear place in everyone's hearts, as did the owners.

After scoping the grounds, and talking with the volunteer vendors, Marta had a moment to check the Pay Q App on her phone. A few more tickets had been sold, but they were still nowhere near the $5,700 they needed to save the restaurant. She also checked her email and social media for any sign from Slate. She knew it was a long shot, but did start to get discouraged when there was zero indication from him he had even gotten her letter, let alone, would show up.

"Where is he, God?"

Nonetheless, the concert was starting soon, and the guests were already arriving. She stationed Katrina and Courtney at the ticket booth to collect the tickets, and eek out any last minute sales at the door, and then went to tell Fozzy and the band to start their first song. This was to set the ambience and hopefully attract anyone driving by to come in and support the show. Just off stage, she had a hawk eyed view of the entire venue. She took a few sips of lemonade as she took in the scene, but her break was short as there was still so much left to do.

Looking out over the field where the guests were sitting on blankets and lawn chairs, she noticed her Grandma Lupita in the crowd. She was sitting with Courtney's dad, and Katrina's mom. This concert was not a secret, but she had not officially told her grandparents that she was putting it on. She did not want to get their hopes up in case they could not pull it off. As much as she wanted to go say hi and welcome to her grandma, that would have to wait. The concert was just starting, and she had an event to run.

Throughout the afternoon, the band had been playing jazzy riffs mixed with familiar marching band songs, and the number of guests coming through the gates had finally tapered off. The audience was seated socially distanced 6 feet apart from each other. Some wore masks, others felt protected by the open air. All were delighted for a good excuse to get out of the house after feeling cooped up for so long because of the pandemic. Families sat in groups together as kids rode their scooters and bikes, and played on the walking path.

The band played so many songs, stretching out their opening act set, trying to keep the energy up in case Slate and The Muggy Hamsters did show up on schedule. With each passing song, everyone knew that the odds of that happening were increasingly slim, but there was no plan B, so the band kept playing.

Marta met up with the other girls behind the ticket booth. At this point, the sun was beginning to set, and reality was becoming clear. Slate was a no show.

"Well, we did an extra $180 at the door, and that is nothing to look down on." said Courtney as she handed the lockbox of cash to Marta.

"I'm so proud of you", said Katrina. "We did sell a lot of tickets."

Marta looked sad, but still had a glimmer of hope and charm in her eyes.

"We are all always going to be best friends, even if we have to come visit you in Alaska, and that is never going to change." Courtney said, forcing a grin.

"We sold a lot of tickets, but I guess we came up short." said Katrina.

"I guess people are probably still scared. Even with social distancing, it's still a scary pandemic, and not everyone is comfortable coming out yet." Courtney said in her kind way.

Marta still just stood there. She was looking at her two best friends, and listening to how invested they were in helping her cause. They cared almost as much as she did. Looking out over the crowd as the band played in the background, Marta really absorbed just how much everyone cared, and it made her a bit emotional.

"You and your family can probably move to one of my Mom's rental properties if you need to in the meantime if things go really south fast, but I knew you probably don't want to..."

"Guys. Thank you" Marta said genuinely, cutting her off. "We tried our best. We raised $797 in three days in a town with a smaller population than Buttongrove. I think we should be proud of ourselves. I love you guys so much."

She leaned in and they all shared a group bear hug, the kind that only your truest best friends can give, and suddenly, everything was brighter.

"We love you so much." said Katrina and Courtney.

They all stepped back, looked at the crowd once more, and then back at each other.

"Well since Slate didn't show-", Katrina began, but then stopped her usual sarcasm to see if she could say it a different way, "I am going to let Fozzy and the band know that they are not only opening, they are now the headlining act."

"I am sure he is going to be thrilled", said Courtney as the girls all giggled.

"I really thought we may have had a miracle," said Marta. "Anyway, we are still going to give a kick ass concert for all of these wonderful people who did show up."

She made a fist, and thrust it in front of her and the girls. "Girl Power?" she asked, in the same way she had asked since they were kids, but now as a confident young woman forging her path forward towards her destiny.

"Girl power!" they all cheered loudly as they bumped their fists and raised them defiantly into the air. No circumstances would be able to control the love they had for each other, and the friendship they shared. So what if things were about to change for them? Their friendship would remain steadfast, and they would ride out this storm like they had so many others, even if they could only communicate via video.

CHAPTER 10

The Brave Rejoice

As the Tafticopa Jazz Band finished the last song of their planned set and put their instruments down to take a break, Marta bravely took the stage to address the crowd. This was supposed to be the time that she was going to introduce Slate and The Muggy Hamsters. He did not show up, but somehow, knowing her friends had her back no matter what, she did not care. She grabbed the mic, took a deep breath, and began to speak confidently with her head held high

"Good evening ladies and gentlemen. Thank you for showing up, masks and all, to our socially distanced, Pandemic safe concert. What some of you didn't know is that the tickets sold were to help my grandparents."

Grandma Lupita beamed with pride when she heard this. She never let Marta know that she knew about the concert. She knew it would be very difficult to raise that amount of money in only 3 days, but still wanted to come and support her granddaughter no matter what. She listened intently.

"They have been a part of this community for a long time, but now, Leon Picante will have to close."

The crowd murmured amongst themselves in a low, collective voice.

"We raised $797, and we couldn't have done it without you. Instead of celebrating a victory, instead, this concert is going to be a celebration of kindness, community, and a celebration of all of you for showing up."

She knew that this was it. She was going to introduce Fozzy and the Tafticopa Jazz Band as the main act of the evening, as her dream of a miracle drifted away on the wind.

"And now without further delay, I present to you..."

Just as Marta began motioning towards stage left at Fozzy and the band to give them their big introduction, music began playing softly from behind the crowd. It was faint, and everyone, including Marta, was surprised and looked around to see where the music was coming from. You could hear a pin drop as the crowd parted, person by person, group by group. When the music got closer, there was no mistaking the riff.

This was Slate's song.

'There Was A Miracle', was being played in just such a way that only one person could. It reached Marta's ears as she squinted and saw their silhouette come into focus against the backdrop of the evening sun. It was Slate and The Muggy Hamsters. They did come, and as they made their way through the crowd, Slate finished Marta's intro by shouting,

"Slate Cruddy, and the Muggy Hamsters!"

The crowd mumbled in anticipation as the band joined Marta on stage.

Slate took the mic from her hand and spoke into it,

"Sorry I'm late, Marta. We were playing a gig in Bakersfield and our tour bus got stuck in a trough in a field. We didn't have wifi for hours. Had to pray our way out of that one"

Marta was in ecstatic disbelief , and turned to the girls offstage. They all smiled and she gave Katrina and Courtney an *I told you so* raised eyebrow. Even Katrina is giddy and happy.

"Anyway, I got your message and heard you needed some help."

He motioned for Scarlet to hand over a huge oversized check she was carrying to Marta that read, 'Pay to the Order of $5,000 to Leon Picante Restaurante'.

"Here you go, Marta," said Scarlet as she smiled and handed it to her.

"We really hope this helps".

She readjusted the strap on her bass guitar as drummer Davey twirled his drumsticks repeatedly in between his fingers. Marta's eyes swelled with emotion.

Slate lowered the mic, and spoke to Marta in his authentic speaking voice as he looked directly into her eyes.

"I told you I owe you a favor. Slate always comes through for my Granites!".

He then resumed his boisterous stage persona and turned to the crowd.

"Plus, we couldn't let Leon Picante close! It's the best salsa in the San Joaquin Valley. Right!?" he asked the audience.

"Right!" they cheered back.

"Pupusas! Pupusas all around! Mmm...and salsa!" said goofy Davey licking his lips.

Fozzy fit Slate with a head mounted microphone, as Slate winked at Marta.

"Now let's really get this show on the road!" He led her off stage as the band began to play full out.

"There was a Miracle
There was a Miracle
And it happened just like that
Just like that
She needed a Miracle
They needed a Miracle

And it happened here in...Taft."

Slate was playing with the lyrics to make them fit this momentous occasion, and to have a little fun. He and The Muggy Hamsters really hammed it up and gave the audience a show they would never forget.

The girls were right off stage when Marta ran down the steps, and they hugged her, giggled, and then all split to go find their parents.

"Oh really, you needed the lights and speakers for a school project?" Mr. Croutonberg asked with a smile on his face.

Courtney just gave him a big hug and said, "Sorry I lied, Daddy, but it was for a good cause." as she sat down next to him on his blanket.

"So you needed the lot to practice interpretative dancing, huh?" asked Mrs. Kobaldini.

Katrina just smiled sheepishly and flashed her mom an awkwardly gleeful look, then sat on her mat. She gave her mom another rare hug. Maybe they would not be so rare anymore. Maybe they got closer through this experience too, and maybe the miracle was not just for Leon Picante but for the whole community. In fact, everyone was hugging each other and sharing laughter and praise.

The girls were caught, and felt slightly guilty for lying, but even their parents could not help but be proud. These girls worked hard to help their friend, and their parents could not be prouder.

Marta was the last to reach her person, Grandma Lupita. She ran towards her as fast as she could with her hair blowing in the wind behind her like a wild horse running through a meadow. With the huge check in hand, she ran fiercely with a renewed spirit and newfound strength, like a boat sailing in the open sea to present the victory to her beloved Abuela.

"We did it grandma, we did it", said Marta.

"You did it, Mihijita. You did it!" cried Lupita.

They both got quiet just for a moment, as they smiled and their eyes were so tight they turned into little slits. They both looked at each other, and then looked up directly into the clouds. At the exact same time they both exclaimed.

"*He* did it!"And they were right.

God had sent them the miracle they prayed for, and the miracle they needed. It was down to the wire, but He came through just in time, as He had so many times before. They both rejoiced loudly with hallelujahs and hosannas, as the music continued to play, giving thanks to God who delivered a true miracle to a brave young woman, in a small little country town, with a population smaller than Buttongrove. Indeed, who delivered a miracle...*un Milagro* in Tafticopa.

~THE END~

<u>Grandma Lupita's World Famous Salsa</u>

This salsa recipe has been passed down for generations. The Caribbean flavors, and Spanish zest make it a go to for corn tortilla chips. It also goes well with burritos, carne asada, enchiladas y mas!

<u>**Ingredients:**</u>

- 2 chopped onions
- 5 large red tomatoes
- ½ fresh picked cilantro
- 4 cloves of garlic
- Juice 2 limes
- Salt
- Creole Seasoning
- 2 jalapeno peppers
- 1 tomatillo
- 1 tablespoon pineapple

<u>Recipe:</u>

Step 1: Gather all ingredients and supplies

Step 2: Combine tomatoes, cilantro, tomatillo, squeezed lime juice, garlic, salt, and onion and onion into a bowl.

Step 3: Mix all ingredients in bowl together

Step 4: Add salt, pineapple juice, and jalapeno

Step 5: Serve and enjoy!

Hebrews 13:5
"Never will I leave you. Never will I forsake you."
John 3:16
"For God so loved the world, that he gave his only begotten Son, that **whosoever** *believeth in him should not perish, but have everlasting life."*

Don't miss out!

Visit the website below and you can sign up to receive emails whenever Vittorio Wyatt Gray publishes a new book. There's no charge and no obligation.

https://books2read.com/r/B-A-QDZVB-TMGUD

BOOKS2READ

Connecting independent readers to independent writers.

About the Author

Vittorio "Wyatt" Gray is an actor, author, husband, and storyteller. Firmly believing that we all belong, he enjoys telling inclusive stories in which everyone matters. A believer, he enjoys telling uplifting and inspirational stories that magnify the importance of kindness and faith.